Ben and the Porcupine

Carol Carrick

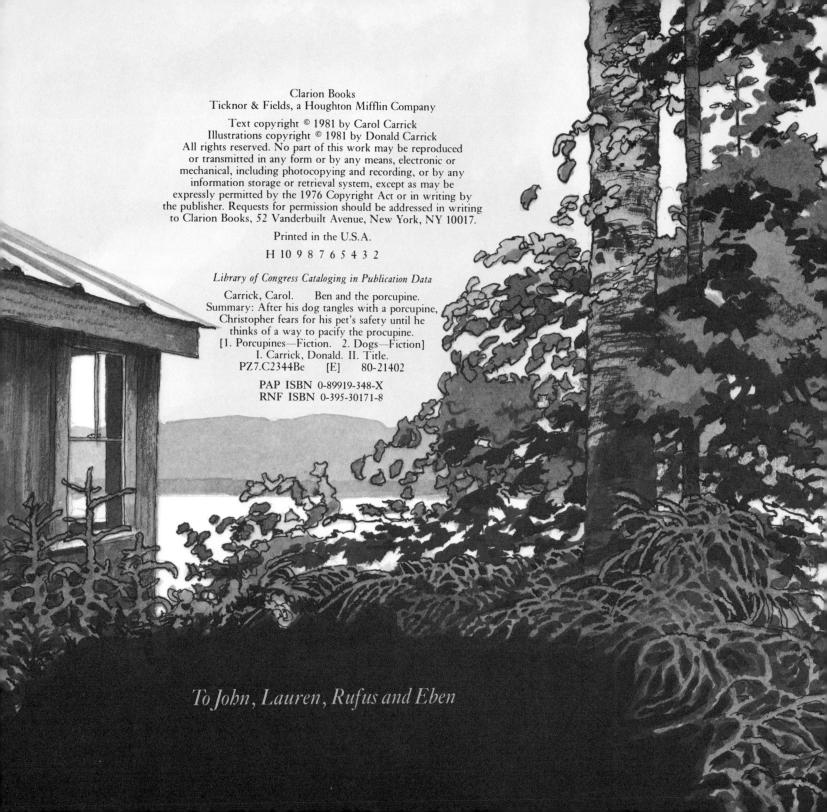

Clarion Books
Ticknor & Fields, a Houghton Mifflin Company

Text copyright © 1981 by Carol Carrick
Illustrations copyright © 1981 by Donald Carrick

Printed in the U.S.A.

H 10 9 8 7 6 5 4 3 2

Library of Congress Cataloging in Publication Data

Carrick, Carol.   Ben and the porcupine.
Summary: After his dog tangles with a porcupine,
Christopher fears for his pet's safety until he
thinks of a way to pacify the procupine.
[1. Porcupines—Fiction. 2. Dogs—Fiction]
I. Carrick, Donald. II. Title.
PZ7.C2344Be   [E]   80-21402

PAP ISBN 0-89919-348-X
RNF ISBN 0-395-30171-8

To John, Lauren, Rufus and Eben

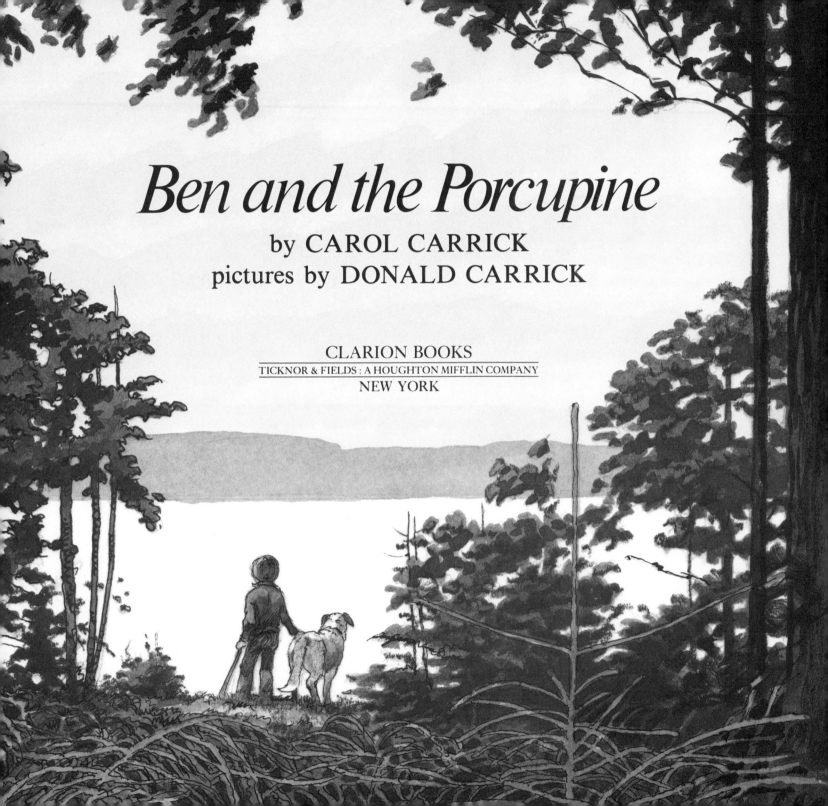

Ben and the Porcupine

by CAROL CARRICK
pictures by DONALD CARRICK

CLARION BOOKS
TICKNOR & FIELDS : A HOUGHTON MIFFLIN COMPANY
NEW YORK

The hayfield was the best place to play ball near the summer cottage. As soon as Christopher swung his bat at the rubber ball, his dog, Ben, took off after it. The ball hit the ground, popped up and rolled. Ben overshot it, and came to a skidding stop.

"Over there! Over there!" Christopher called, pointing to the ball.

Ben found it, carried it back in his mouth, and dropped it at Christopher's feet. The dog pranced in front of him, waiting for the next hit.

Christopher swung and missed. But Ben tore off across the field. Soon he slowed and stopped. Then he looked back at Christopher, his head cocked as if to ask where the ball went. When Christopher laughed, Ben trotted back with his tail wagging and his tongue hanging out in a doggy grin. He didn't seem to know that the joke was on him.

Christopher threw the ball up again and swung hard. "Wow! A good one!" he shouted. "Get it, Ben!"

Ben was stalking something in the little brook that ran through the meadow, probably a frog.

"Hey, Ben. You're supposed to pay attention. Where's the ball?"

But Ben had lost interest in the game.

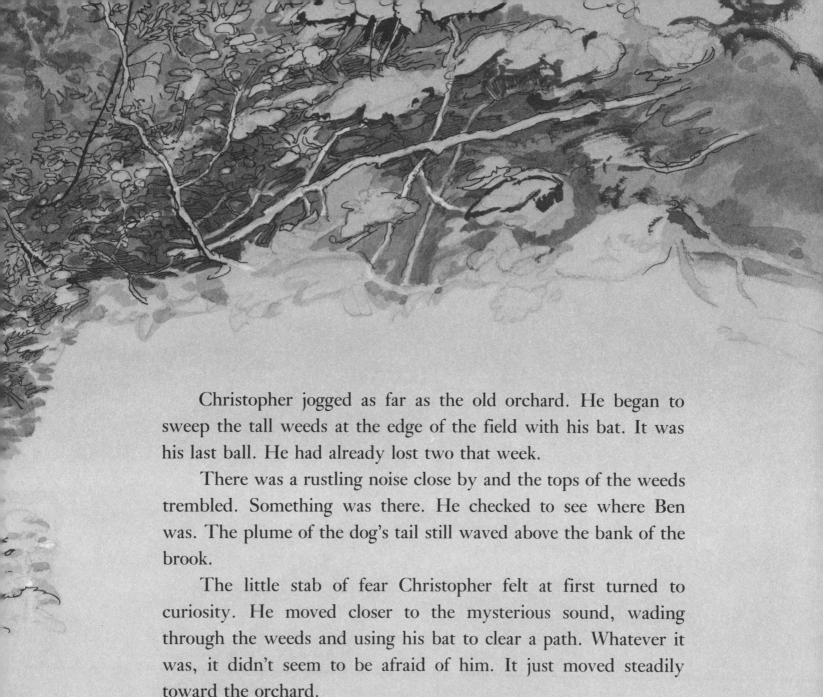

Christopher jogged as far as the old orchard. He began to sweep the tall weeds at the edge of the field with his bat. It was his last ball. He had already lost two that week.

There was a rustling noise close by and the tops of the weeds trembled. Something was there. He checked to see where Ben was. The plume of the dog's tail still waved above the bank of the brook.

The little stab of fear Christopher felt at first turned to curiosity. He moved closer to the mysterious sound, wading through the weeds and using his bat to clear a path. Whatever it was, it didn't seem to be afraid of him. It just moved steadily toward the orchard.

As it came into the clearing under the trees, Christopher could see the greyish-black animal. It was pretty big, bigger than a cat. And it seemed to swell even bigger before his eyes. It had raised a halo of quills over its back. A porcupine! Christopher had only seen one once before.

The porcupine started to climb one of the apple trees. For something that looked so clumsy it was a good climber.

Christopher heard Ben's big feet crashing through the weeds. "Oh, no," he thought. "There's going to be trouble." Ben never caught anything, but he still acted as if he was a big hunter.

When Ben saw the porcupine he barked, but the porcupine seemed to ignore him. It just curled up in a crotch of the tree. The dog stood up on his hind legs and scratched at the tree, whimpering with excitement.

Christopher went back to the edge of the field and called, slapping his knees. "C'mon, Ben! C'mere boy!"

But Ben wouldn't come. Instead, he ran from one side of the tree to the other, barking.

Christopher ran home to get help. By the time he reached the driveway where his father was getting out of the van, he was out of breath.

"Dad!" Christopher panted. "There's a porcupine in one of the apple trees."

"Really?" his father answered. "Here, help me unload this firewood."

"But Ben's going to get stuck by the quills."

"Not unless he's learned how to climb trees," Christopher's father said, carrying an armload of wood toward the house.

"Don't you think we should tie Ben up?" Christopher asked, running behind his father's big strides.

His father threw the wood in a pile. "The woods are full of animals. And we're not going to keep that dog tied. He's just going to have to learn about porcupines."

"But, Dad . . . "

"Bring up the firewood and I'll show you how to split kindling with an ax."

Still, Christopher was relieved to see Ben come home before they had finished unloading the wood.

After dark, Christopher lay in bed, listening to Ben who was out on the dirt road, barking. Ben did that every night until he was ready to come in. Christopher's father said Ben was scaring away the ghosts. But tonight Christopher knew that something real, something dangerous was out there.

Christopher was dreaming that Ben could catch a ball in his mouth and throw it back, too, when a cry from outside woke him. Then he heard someone rush to the front door.

Christopher left his bed and went to the living room. He shivered, blinking in the bright light at his mother, who held open the screen door. Outside, his father shone a flashlight into the night.

"Ben!" Christopher cried as the dog appeared out of the darkness. Long quills bristled around his nose like a horrible comic moustache.

"Poor guy. Looks like he tangled with that porcupine you told me about," his father said.

Ben stood there, his head drooping, and looked at them with a shamed expression.

Angry tears filled Christopher's eyes. "Didn't I tell you he was going to get hurt?"

He put his arm around the dog's neck and pulled out one of the loose quills. Ben squealed and squirmed free from his grip.

"He's not going to let you take the rest out," said his mother. She looked at Christopher's father. "What are we going to do?"

His father examined the barbed hook on the end of the quill. "You'd better call the vet," he said. "He'll be able to put Ben to sleep while he works on him."

But when his mother called, she learned that the vet would probably be gone most of the night, taking care of a farmer's sick cow.

Ben whimpered and rubbed at his face with one paw.

"We've got to help him, Dad," Christopher pleaded. "We can't let him suffer like this."

"I'll help you hold him," his mother offered.

Christopher's father got his pliers and carefully worked the tiny hooks out of the dog's nose. Ben struggled and yipped. Christopher buried his face in the dog's fur and tried to shut out Ben's pitiful cries as he held him tight.

At last it was over. Ben bolted into Christopher's room and crawled under the bed. Christopher wriggled under after him. He laid his head on Ben's trembling shoulder, patting him and talking softly. The dog soon fell asleep, and Christopher crept back into his own bed.

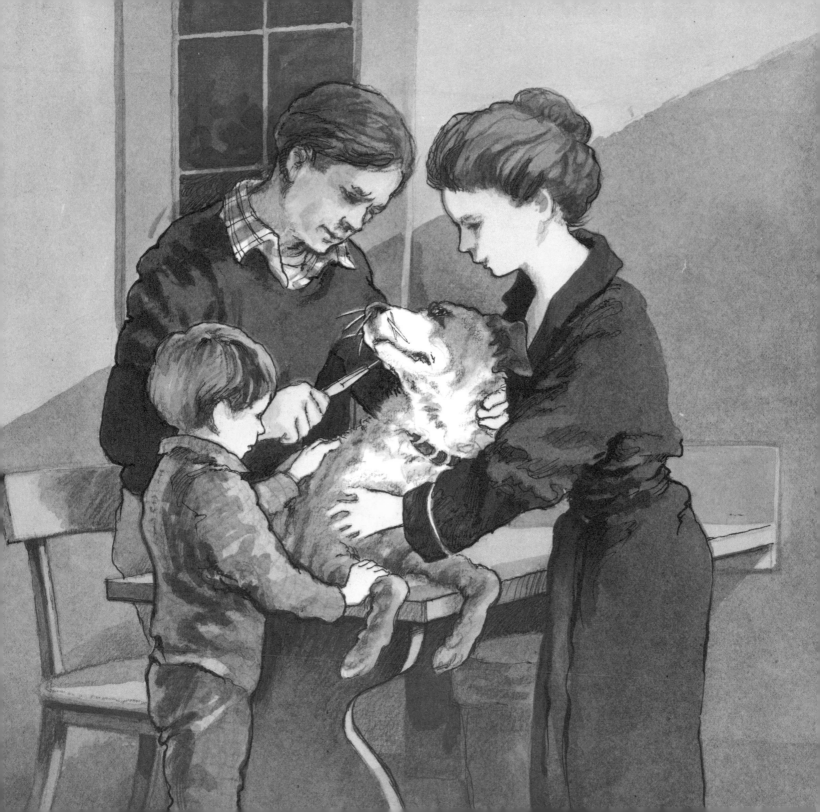

In the morning Christopher heard his father outside splitting logs. When Christopher joined him, his father held up the ax.

"This was left outside," he said. "And guess what happened to it."

Christopher looked at the ax. The end of the handle had been chewed.

"That's what the porcupine was doing here last night," his father said.

But Christopher still didn't understand.

"He was attracted to the salt that the sweat from your hands left on the wood," his father explained.

Then Christopher spotted Ben lying in the sun. "Poor Ben. How's your nose?" he asked.

Ben rolled on his back and greeted Christopher by flopping his tail against the ground. Christopher kneeled down to scratch the dog's belly.

"He looks fine this morning," Christopher's father said. "Let's hope he learned his lesson the first time."

Christopher's mouth dropped open in surprise. "You mean it could happen to Ben again?" he cried, standing up. "Oh, no!"

"That's right," his father answered. "Some dogs never seem to catch on. I had a dog once that just wouldn't let porcupines alone. One time he even came home with quills in his tongue."

Christopher shuddered. "But Dad, Ben thinks it's his job to guard the house. If the porcupine comes back, Ben may not know what it is in the dark."

His father shrugged. "I'm sorry, but there's not much we can do about it. The porcupine is defending itself."

Christopher began to stack the wood that was already cut. He didn't say any more about it to his father, but he couldn't help thinking about the porcupine he had seen and the quills buried in Ben's tender nose.

After the job was finished he grabbed his bat and went back to the orchard to look for his ball. When Ben tried to follow, Christopher shut him in the house. As he left he could hear Ben whining and scratching at the door.

Christopher walked carefully when he reached the tall weeds. He was afraid of bumping into the porcupine. After a while he got tired of looking for the ball. He began to swing at the apples lying under the trees.

It felt lonesome out there without Ben's company. His dad was right. He couldn't keep Ben locked up forever. Ben wouldn't be happy that way.

The apples gave Christopher an idea. Before he went home he
left a gift under the porcupine's tree. Maybe the porcupine would
like it so much he would stay away from the house—and from
Ben.

That night, after dark, Christopher lay in bed listening to Ben bark in the moonlight. "Oh please stay away, porcupine! Stay away!" he whispered in the darkness.

Christopher tried to think of something else, but every time he heard a rustle, his body tensed. Several times he got out of bed and strained to see what was in the woods outside his window. He wondered if his plan to keep the porcupine in the orchard would work. It had to.

It wasn't until a beam of moonlight had crept all the way across the floor, and shone on his pillow, that he heard a 'woof' at the front door. The door was opened and he heard his father say,

"Scared all the ghosts, did you?"

Christopher smiled to himself as he listened to the click of nails coming toward his room on the wooden floor. Ben was all right.

"Good night, Ben," he called softly as the dog settled down on his rug in the corner of the room.

Christopher rolled over. Now he felt sleepy.

Tomorrow he planned to go back to the orchard. Under one of the trees there was a baseball bat. He wanted to check the handle. It wouldn't really matter if it had a few toothmarks. Summer was almost over anyway—and so was the season for baseball.